The Lazy Man
소가 된 게으름뱅이

The
Spring of Youth
젊어지는 샘물

HOLLYM

The Lazy Man

Once upon a time, in a small village, there lived a young man who spent his whole day doing nothing.

Even during the busiest part of the farming season, he just slept and snored. Finally, his wife could no longer keep her temper under control. In her loudest voice she ordered him, "Get out into the field and do some work."

The man just rolled over on his side and frowned.

"Don't bother me," he said. "Why do you keep bothering me when I'm so tired and sleepy?"

소가 된 게으름뱅이

옛날, 어느 마을에 빈둥빈둥 놀기만 하는 사나이가 있었습니다.

바쁜 농사철이 되어도 사나이는 쿨쿨 낮잠만 잤습니다.

하루는, 참다 못한 아내가 사나이에게 화를 내며 말했습니다.

"여보! 밭에 나가 일 좀 해요."

방바닥에 뒹굴던 사나이는 얼굴을 찡그리며 대꾸했습니다.

"귀찮게 굴지 마오. 졸음이 밀려오는데 무슨 일을 하라는 거요."

His wife became angrier and angrier. "How can you spend all day sleeping?" she complained. "Even our children go out to the fields to work. If you keep on loafing like this, our whole family will starve to death."

The man held his hands over his ears and grumbled, "I'd be better off if I left home."

"Then why don't you leave!" yelled his wife.

The man jumped up and ran off.

The wife was so astonished at his speed that she just stood there with her mouth open.

아내는 더욱 화가 났습니다.

"당신은 어떻게 매일 놀기만 하죠? 아이들도 땀을 뻘뻘 흘리며 일을 거든답니다! 이러다가 우리 식구는 모두 굶어 죽겠어요."

사나이는 귀를 틀어 막았습니다.

"차라리 내가 집을 나가는 게 편하겠소."

"어디 마음대로 하시구료!"

아내는 화가 나서 쏘아붙였습니다.

그러자 사나이는 벌떡 일어나, 집을 나갔습니다.

아내는 어처구니가 없어서 멍하니 보고만 있었습니다.

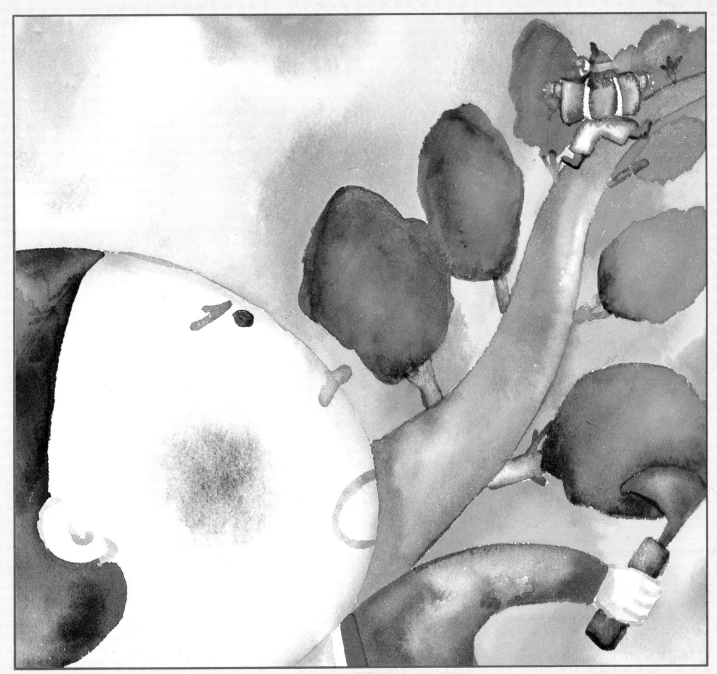

Walking down the road, the man saw an ox chewing its cud. The ox was half asleep, resting in the midday sun. "That ox is very lucky," he thought. "If only I were an ox...."

Then he continued his stroll toward the ridge of a nearby mountain. When he reached the ridge he saw a shanty with a straw roof. The house was so old that it was barely standing. Inside the house an old man was very busy making something. The lazy man was so curious that he stopped to look.

길을 가던 사나이는 그늘에서 되새김질을 하며 꿈벅꿈벅 졸고 있는 소를 만났습니다.

"그 소 팔자 한번 좋구나! 나도 소나 되었으면…….."

물끄러미 소를 바라보던 사나이는 산등성이로 발길을 옮겼습니다.

산등성이로 접어드니, 다 쓰러져가는 초가집 한 채가 있었습니다.

초가집에서는 웬 노인이 열심히 무언가를 만들고 있었습니다.

그냥 지나치려던 사나이는 문득 궁금한 생각이 들었습니다.

9

"Excuse me," he said to the old man, "what are you making?"

The old man held up a mask and grunted, "I'm making an ox-head mask."

"Ah!" the lazy man laughed. "An ox-head mask! Why would anyone work so hard to make such a worthless thing? It would be better to sleep."

The old man laughed, much heartier than the lazy man had.

"여보시오 노인, 지금 만들고 있는 게 뭐요."

"소머리 탈이요."

노인은 괴상한 물건을 들어 보이며 퉁명스레 말했습니다.

"소머리 모양의 탈이구료. 그런 쓸모 없는 걸 만들다니, 차라리 낮잠이나 잘 일이지……."

사나이가 빈정거렸습니다.

"허허허허……, 이 세상에 쓸 데 없는 일을 하는 사람은 없다오."

노인은 너털웃음을 지으며 말했습니다.

11

"There is no such thing in this world as work that is worthless."

"Is that what you think?" scoffed the lazy man. "Well, in that case, good luck to you and your noble task."

As the lazy man turned to go, the old man grumbled softly, "This mask might come in handy for someone who doesn't want to work."

"Come in handy, you say? How?"

"If you really want to know, why don't you try it on?" the old man said and quickly placed the mask on the lazy man's face.

At the same time, the old man picked up the leather strap he had been hiding and tied it to the iron ring that went through the nose of the ox-mask.

"흥, 열심히 일이나 하시구료."
사나이가 코웃음을 치며 막 돌아서는데, 노인이 혼잣말로 중얼거렸습니다.
"일하기 싫어하는 사람이 이 탈을 쓰면 좋은 수가 생기지."
그 말에 귀가 솔깃해진 사나이는 발걸음을 멈추고 돌아보았습니다.
"좋은 수라니, 그게 대체 뭡니까?"

"궁금하면 이 탈을 한번 써 보라구!"
노인은 탈을 번쩍 들어서 사나이에게 덥석 씌웠습니다.
그리고 숨기고 있던 가죽끈을 집어들어 소탈의 코에 있는 고리에 묶었습니다.

No matter how hard the lazy man pulled and pulled, the mask would not come off. "Please help me get this thing off," he begged. "It's very hot." But his words sounded very strange. They were very low and gruff, like the noise an ox makes. They sounded like, "Moo! Moo!

The lazy man ran around in circles, bawling like an ox. "Moo! Moo!" he said.

Then the old man pulled on the leather strap and started to lead the lazy man away, mask and all.

그러자 소머리 탈은 사나이의 머리에 찰싹 달라붙어 떨어질 줄을 몰랐습니다.

사나이는 탈을 벗으려고 낑낑대며 소리쳤습니다.

"제발 이 탈 좀 벗겨 주시오. 더워서 못 살겠어요."

"음메 음메……."

사나이는 소처럼 울면서 맴을 돌았습니다.

이상하게도 사나이의 목소리는 낮고 거친 소의 울음소리가 되어 나왔습니다.

사나이는 기가 막혀서 엉엉 울었습니다.

노인은 소가 된 사나이에게 고삐를 걸어 어디론가 끌고 갔습니다.

Before long, the lazy man heard the sounds of men laughing and arguing. He realized that he was in the market where oxen were bought and sold. He was inside a fence with other oxen.

Then he heard the old man talking to a farmer. The farmer gave the old man some money. The old man said, "Remember, make sure that you keep him away from the radish fields, if he eats radish, he will die at once." "Some oxen are sure peculiar," the farmer said, shaking his head in wonderment. Then he led his newly purchased ox home.

사람들이 와글와글 떠드는 소리에 사나이는 자기가 장터에 와 있다는 것을 알아차렸습니다.

사나이는 많은 소들 틈에 끼어 있었습니다.

노인은 사나이를 어느 농부에게 팔아 넘기면서 말했습니다.

"이 소는 무우를 먹으면 곧 죽으니, 절대로 무우밭에 못 가게 하시오."

"참 별난 소도 다 있네."

농부는 고개를 갸웃거리다가, 소를 몰고 집으로 갔습니다.

It was the hottest part of a very hot day. "Hurry up! Hurry up! You stupid ox, why are you so lazy?" The farmer yelled as he hit the back of the lazy man with a big stick.

"I'm not an ox," the lazy man complained. "I'm a man in an ox-mask." But his words sounded like "Moo! Moo!" and the farmer only hit him harder.

The man stopped mooing and thought to himself, "I guess this is my punishment for being so lazy...."

All day long, lazy man worked and worked without even a minute's rest. He even had to pull a heavy wagon.

햇볕이 '쨍쨍' 내리쬐는 한낮이었습니다.

"이러 이러! 이 놈의 소는 왜 이리도 게으른가."

밭갈이를 하던 농부는 소가 된 사나이의 등을 철썩철썩 때렸습니다.

"나는 소가 아니라 사람이오!"

지칠대로 지친 사나이가 아무리 큰 소리로 울부짖어도 그 소리는 '음메 음메' 하고 났으며, 농부는 더 세게 채찍질을 했습니다.

'그동안 게으름만 피우고 살았더니 이렇게 큰 벌을 받는구나!'

사나이는 조금도 쉬지 못하고 힘든 일을 해야만 했습니다. 심지어는 무거운 수레까지도 끌어야 했습니다.

Night came. The lazy man was finally taken to his pen. Although he was very tired, he could not sleep. All he could do was cry and think about his family. "I wonder how my wife and children are?"he asked himself and cried even harder.

"I'd rather be dead than an ox," he said to himself. "That's it!" he suddenly blurted out, remembering what he had heard the old man tell the farmer at the market. "If I eat some radishes, I'll die!"

With what little strength he had left, the lazy man broke out of the pen.

밤이 되었습니다.
　사나이는 외양간에서 겨우 쉬게 되었습니다.
　피곤했지만 잠을 잘 수가 없었습니다. 식구들 생각에 눈물을 흘리는 일밖엔 아무것도 할 수 없었습니다.
　"아내와 아이들은 잘 있을까?"

'이렇게 소가 되어 사는 것보다는 차라리 죽는 게 낫지.'
　그러자 장터에서 노인이 한 말이 퍼뜩 떠올랐습니다.
　"그렇다! 무우를 먹으면 죽는다!"
　사나이는 살금살금 외양간에서 기어나왔습니다.

He went over to where the farmer had a basket of radishes and pulled out several. "So it is time to die," he said. Then he closed his eyes and bit down hard on a radish.

All of a sudden the ox - head mask fell off his face. "What's happening?" he wondered out. He was so happy he did not know what to do. Then the ox hide fell off his back and he was a man again.

At that moment the farmer came out to feed the animals. "Hey! What's going on here?" he shouted at the lazy man.

사나이는 무우 몇 개를 뽑아서 외양간으로 돌아왔습니다.

"이젠 죽는구나."

사나이는 두 눈을 질끈 감고 무우를 으적으적 썹어먹었습니다.

그런데 갑자기 찰싹 달라붙어 있던 소머리 탈이 스르르 벗겨졌습니다.

'아니, 이게 웬일까?'

사나이는 기뻐서 어쩔 줄을 몰랐습니다.

등에 걸친 소가죽까지 훨훨 벗어 던진 사나이는 다시 사람이 되었습니다.

그 때 마침, 여물을 주러 나온 농부가 사나이를 보고 '으앗' 하고 소리를 질렀습니다.

The lazy man was so happy to be a man again that he explained the whole story to the farmer.

Then, with a happy heart, the lazy man headed for his house. When he got home, he set to work in the field and worked all day.

His wife did not know the reason for the big change in her husband. But from that day on he worked harder than anyone and became known as the hardest working man in the village.

사나이는 농부에게 지나간 이야기를 모두 해주었습니다.

그리고는 기쁜 마음으로 바삐 집을 향해 떠났습니다.

집으로 돌아온 사나이는 하루종일 밭에 나가 열심히 일했습니다.

아내는 영문을 몰라 어리둥절했습니다.

그 뒤에 사나이는 어느 누구보다 열심히 일하는 사람이 되었습니다.

The Spring of Youth

Once upon a time, in a mountain village,   there lived a good-hearted old man and his wife. They were very happy but sometimes they were sad because they had no children.   For that reason, they always felt a little lonely.

Every day, the old man went into the mountains to cut wood to sell as firewood in the market. But cutting wood was very hard work for someone his age.

젊어지는 샘물

옛날, 조그만 산골 마을에 마음씨 착한 할아버지와 할머니가 살았습니다.

할아버지와 할머니는 오순도순 정답게 지냈지만 자식이 없어서 언제나 마음 한 구석이 쓸쓸했습니다.

할아버지는 이른 아침부터 산에 올라가 나무를 해서 장에 내다 팔았습니다.

나이가 많은 할아버지는 나무를 하는 일이 무척 힘들었습니다.

One summer day, which seemed no different from any day, the old man went into the mountains to cut wood, as he always did.

Soon the sound of his ax going "chop, chop" filled the forest.

Suddenly, the old man heard the beautiful sound of a bird singing. "That is the most lovely sound I ever heard!" he exclaimed. So, just for a moment, he stopped chopping and wiped the sweat from his brow.

Then the sweet song of the bird became even more wonderful. "Tweet, tweet, tweet, tweet."

The song was so beautiful that the old man wanted to see the bird.

He put down his ax and went over the hill, toward the sound.

어느 여름날이었습니다.

할아버지는 여느 때처럼 나무를 하러 산으로 올라갔습니다.

'뚝딱 뚝딱' 산속은 할아버지의 나무 찍는 소리로 가득 찼습니다.

그런데 어디선가 고운 새소리가 들려 왔습니다.

"처음 듣는 고운 소리구나!"

할아버지는 일손을 멈추고 이마에 송송 맺힌 땀을 쓱 닦았습니다.

"삐오로롱 삐오로롱"

할아버지는 노래 소리가 너무도 아름다워 새가 보고 싶어졌습니다.

할아버지는 도끼를 내려 놓고 노래 소리가 들리는 언덕을 향해 갔습니다.

A white bird was perched on the branch of an oak tree. The old man had never seen a bird like it.

Tired from his morning's work, the old man sighed, "Phew! I think I'll rest here a moment."

The bird sang on and on for a little while. Then it fluttered over to a tree a little farther off and started singing a different tune.

The old man wanted to hear more, so he walked to the tree the bird was in and sat down.

Shortly after the man sat down, the bird stopped singing and flew to a different tree. Then he started to sing again. The old man wandered over to where the bird was in order to listen better.

The bird kept going deeper and deeper into the woods.

할아버지가 고개를 들고 둘러보니, 참나무 가지에 처음 보는 예쁜 새가 앉아서 지저귀고 있었습니다.

"휴우, 좀 쉬었다 하자."

할아버지는 그루터기에 걸터앉아 담뱃대에 불을 붙였습니다.

새는 한참 동안 즐겁게 노래하더니 다른 나뭇가지로 푸드득 날아갔습니다.

할아버지는 노래가 더 듣고 싶어서 새가 있는 곳으로 자리를 옮겼습니다.

그러자 새는 더 멀리 있는 가지로 날아가 버렸습니다.

할아버지는 자기도 모르는 사이에 새의 노래에 이끌려 깊숙한 골짜기에 이르게 되었습니다.

Morning became afternoon. The old man suddenly shook his head in bewilderment. "What have I done!" he cried. "Why have I wandered so far? Where am I?"

At that moment, the bird fluttered over to where the old man stood scratching his head. It flew around the man's head two or three times, then landed beside a nearby spring.

The old man was very thirsty from following the bird so far into the forest. He bent down to the spring and cupped his hands in the water. Then he took a long, deep drink. "This is very refreshing!" he said to himelf between swallows. "It's as sweet as honey!"

But then he felt very lightheaded. "Why do I feel so strange?" he wondered. "I feel like I've been drinking wine."

So the old man lay down on a flat rock and fell fast asleep.

아침이 지나 오후가 되었습니다.
'내가 왜 여기까지 왔을까?'
할아버지는 고개를 갸웃거렸습니다.
그 때 할아버지가 뒤쫓던 새가 푸드득 날아와 앉았습니다.
새가 날아와 앉은 나무 밑에는 맑은 샘물이 퐁퐁 솟고 있었습니다.
마침 목이 마르던 할아버지는 샘물로 달려가 꿀꺽 꿀꺽 물을 마셨습니다.
'어, 참 시원하다! 꿀물같이 달구나.'
그런데 샘물을 마신 할아버지는 얼얼하게 취하는 것 같았습니다.
"내가 왜 이럴까? 술을 마신 것처럼 기분이 좋구나."
할아버지는 샘물 옆에 있는 평평한 바위에 누워 쿨쿨 잠이 들었습니다.

The day grew dark and the old man did not return home.
His wife became very worried. "Surely he hasn't run into a wild
animal," she told herself.

When it became very late, the old woman went all around
the neighborhood in search of her husband.

But he was sleeping soundly on a rock in the deep, deep forest.
He did not wake up until the middle of the night.

"Why have I been sleeping here?" the old man sighed. Quickly
he started walking back down the mountain.

늦도록 할아버지가 돌아오지 않자, 집에서 기다리던 할머니는 걱정이 되었습니다.

'혹시 사나운 짐승이라도 만난 게 아닐까?'

할머니는 부랴부랴 할아버지를 찾아 나섰습니다.

그러나 할아버지는 아무 것도 모르고 산 속에서 깊은 잠에 빠져 있었습니다.

할아버지는 한밤중이 넘어서야 부시시 일어났습니다.

'내가 왜 이런 곳에서 자고 있었을까?'

할아버지는 서둘러 산을 내려왔습니다.

After looking here and there for her husband, the old woman finally went to the next-door neighbor's house. "My husband is lost in the mountains," she said. "I'm afraid something has happened to him. Can you help me find him?"

But the man next door was known throughout the village as a very selfish person. "Look here!" he said in an angry voice. "It's the middle of the night. It's no time to go looking for someone. I won't go." So the old woman set out on the mountain path alone.

She had not gone far when her husband came striding toward her.

여기저기 할아버지를 찾아 다니던 할머니는 이웃집 영감에게 가서 말했습니다.

"우리 영감이 여태 돌아오지 않았어요. 아마 깊은 산 속에 있는 모양이니 함께 가서 좀 찾아 주세요."

"여보시오, 이 밤중에 어딜 가서 사람을 찾는다는 거요. 난 못 가겠소."

이웃집 영감은 심술 사납고 욕심 많기로 소문난 사람이었습니다.

할머니는 하는 수 없이 혼자서 산길을 올라갔습니다.

그리고 얼마 지나지 않아 성큼성큼 걸어오는 할아버지를 만났습니다

They hugged each other until they cried. Then they walked back home together, arm in arm.

Inside, the old woman lit a lamp. As soon as the room lit up, she almost fainted. "Who are you?"

"It's your husband, of course," the old man said. "What's the matter? Is something wrong?"

The old woman backed slowly away from the old man, "Are you some kind of ghost?" she said in a faint voice. "Your wrinkled face has become smooth. You look like the man I married forty years ago."

"What?" the old man said as he touched his face with his hands.

It was just as his wife had said. He was no longer an old man—he was young.

할머니와 할아버지는 함께 집으로 돌아왔습니다.

방으로 들어온 할머니는 소스라치게 놀랐습니다.

"왜 그러시오. 할멈. 뭐가 잘못 됐소?"

할아버지가 어리둥절하여 물었습니다. "내가 도깨비한테 홀렸나?"

할머니는 주춤주춤 물러섰습니다.

"쭈글쭈글하던 영감 얼굴이 청년처럼 반반해졌구료."

할아버지도 놀라서 얼른 얼굴을 더듬어 보았습니다.

아내가 말하는 그대로였습니다. 할아버지는 어느새 청년이 되어 있었습니다.

He sat down to think. "How can this be?" he wondered. Suddenly, he slapped his knee. "I know what happened!" he said, laughing. "It must be the spring water I drank."

The old woman was very puzzled. All smiles, her husband told her all about the day's events.

When he was finished, she almost cried. "I'm glad that this wonderful thing has happened to you. But everyone will think it strange that you have such an old wife."

The man just laughed louder. "That's easy! Come back to the fountain with me. Then you can become young again, too. We'll both be young! Then nobody will think it strange that you are married to such a young man."

As soon as it became light enough the next day, the man took his old wife to the spring.

'어떻게 이럴 수가!'
곰곰히 생각을 하던 할아버지는 갑자기 무릎을 탁 쳤습니다.
"옳거니, 그 샘물 때문이로구나!"
할아버지는 영문을 몰라 멍하니 쳐다보는 할머니에게 낮에 있었던 일을 차근차근 이야기해 주었습니다.
"당신이 이렇게 젊으니, 남들이 우리를 보면 이상하게 여기겠죠?"
할머니가 한숨을 쉬며 말했습니다.
"여보, 당신도 그 샘물을 먹도록 합시다. 그러면 당신도 다시 젊어질테고, 아무도 당신이 젊은이와 결혼했다고 이상하게 생각하지 않을 게 아니오?"
이튿날 날이 밝자, 할아버지와 할머니는 이상한 샘물을 찾아갔습니다.

She drank a few of the water and fell asleep. When she awoke, her husband was sitting by her side. And she was a pretty, young woman again.

The young couple lived together even more happily than they had before. But the mean neighbor next door became unbearably jealous of them. "I want to lose my wrinkles and white hair, too. I want to be young again and live a long life, too," he fumed.

He could not stand it any longer. So he hurried over to the young couple's house. "You must tell me," he shouted, "How did you become young again ? "

After the couple told him about the spring deep in the woods, the selfish neighbor hurried to the mountains alone, mumbling to himself.

He did not come back that day or the next.

할머니는 샘물 몇 모금을 마시고 잠이 들었습니다.

잠에서 깨어나자 할머니는 다시 예쁜 새색시가 되어 있었습니다.

할아버지와 할머니는 젊은 부부가 되어 즐겁게 지냈습니다.

그것을 본 이웃집 영감은 샘이 나서 가만히 있을 수가 없었습니다.

'나도 젊어져서 오래오래 살아야지.'

이웃집 영감은 부리나케 할아버지를 찾아와 젊어지는 샘물에 대해 꼬치꼬치 캐물었습니다.

그리고는 허둥지둥 산으로 올라갔습니다.

이웃집 영감은 며칠이 지나도록 돌아오지 않았습니다.

The young man and the young woman became worried, so they went to look for him.

When they reached the spring, they found only a little puddle of water.

Then they heard a very loud, high-pitched cry coming from a nearby rock.

When they looked, they saw a baby on top of their neighbor's clothes.

"Ha! Ha! Ha!" laughed the man. "As our neighbor drank so much of the spring water, he became a baby again." They raised him as though he were their very own. With their kind, loving care, the baby grew into a nice, helpful young boy.

할아버지와 할머니는 걱정이 되어 이웃집 영감을 찾아 나섰습니다.

이윽고 젊어지는 샘물까지 찾아간 두 사람은 아주 작은 옹달샘을 발견했습니다. 그 때, 바위 옆에서 '응아 응아'하는, 아기의 울음소리가 들려왔습니다.

이상하게 여긴 두 사람이 샘물 옆에 있는 바위를 보니, 이웃집 영감의 옷을 입은 아기가 울고 있었습니다.

"하하하, 이웃집 영감이 샘물을 너무 많이 마셔서 아기가 됐구료."

젊어진 할아버지와 할머니는 아기를 데리고 집으로 돌아왔습니다.

욕심 많은 영감은 아기가 되어 착하게 무럭무럭 자랐습니다.